Board Games

Collect all the books in the Luna Bay *series*

Luna Bay
a ♥ ROXY GiRL series

BOOK SEVEN

Board
Games

by Cathy East Dubowski

HarperEntertainment
An Imprint of HarperCollinsPublishers

LUNA BAY: BOARD GAMES. Copyright © 2004 by Quiksilver, Inc. All rights reserved. Printed in the United States of America. No part of this book may be used or reproduced in any manner whatsoever without written permission except in the case of brief quotations embodied in critical articles and reviews. For information address HarperCollins Publishers Inc., 10 East 53rd Street, New York, NY 10022.

HarperCollins books may be purchased for educational, business, or sales promotional use. For information please write: Special Markets Department, HarperCollins Publishers Inc., 10 East 53rd Street, New York, NY 10022.

FIRST EDITION

Designed by Susan Sanguily

ISBN 0-06-058912-4

WBC/OPM 10 9 8 7 6 5 4 3 2 1

Acknowledgments

With gratitude to Hope Innelli, Mabel Zorzano, Susan Sanguily, Matt Jacobson, Diana Krupa, and everyone at HarperEntertainment and Quiksilver Entertainment; to my wonderful editor, Jeffery S. McGraw, who inspires me to keep soul-surfing the language even when those big monster waves start crashing all around and whose excellent editing rescues me from all the wipeouts; and to Mark, my surfing buddy—thank you for everything.

Board Games

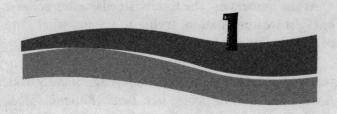

Morning, Luna Bay

The world is a black-and-white movie. There's just enough light to see objects in various shades of gray. The smooth, empty stretch of beach. The whitecaps of the waves. A forgotten pair of flip-flops near an empty lifeguard stand. A fishing boat so far out it looks like a toy. Rae waits for the sun to rise and paint in the colors.

The beach belongs to her this morning. She digs both feet into the cool, gritty sand, embraces the sound of the waves hitting the shore, as steady as a heartbeat. The water playfully reaches for her toes before flowing back to join the game. The salty air smells brand new.

Rae feels as if she's sharing a secret.

It's a little chilly this morning, so she jogs up and down in place, glad she wore her wet suit. She rolls her shoulders, reaches for the sky, stretches her hamstrings, warming up as she eyes that imaginary line called the horizon, where the sky is lightest, promising that a new day is about to begin.

As she limbers up, she listens, smells, tastes, sees—a one-girl weather station, trying to predict what kind of day it's going to be.

The ocean has even more moods than a sixteen-year-old girl. *How do you feel today?* she silently asks. *Rowdy and busting loose, like Luna, Kanani, Isobel, Cricket, and I do when we escape from school and hit the beach? Or troubled and angry, like Mom whenever Dad calls . . . or doesn't?*

Rae shakes her head, trying not to go there. *Just think about the waves* . . . Then she grins. No, today the ocean is just happy, she decides. No stress, but up, full of energy, as if anything were possible.

This is where I'm supposed to be, Rae thinks. She loves surfing with her girlfriends, loves to compete, to sharpen her skills against the challenge of another good surfer.

But sometimes she loves to be out here all alone. It's like meditating, with nothing to prove.

If I could just get Mom out here this time of day, she thinks. *If she could see the ocean like this, maybe she'd understand what it does to me. For me. If I could just get her up on a board one time and let her feel the rush of that moment when you catch a ride on a good wave and start to fly. . . .*

Yeah, right! Rae laughs as she picks up the coffee at her feet and brushes the sand from the paper cup. Her

mom only gets horses. Thinks surfing is goofing off—
something her mom never does.

Other thoughts trespass on these thoughts. Rae's got
a big math test coming up. *Probably should be home
studying for it right now.* And she's worried about her
parents: she'd tried to believe their separation was one
of those midlife, freak-out, grown-up kind of things.
She'd wished on stars, over other people's birthday can-
dles, hoping she'd wake up one day and everything
would be back to normal. But the weeks were turning
into months now, and it was getting harder to pretend.

And her dad—she hasn't heard from him in a while.
Is he so busy in Chicago that he forgets that she and
her sister, Sherri, need him, too?

Suddenly—it's almost impossible to see it happen—
the sky begins to lighten. Rae feels her blood quicken.
Soon—in mere seconds, it seems—the light turns pink,
like liquid blush spilled across the edge of the earth.

Dawn.

Rae crosses her ankles and sinks onto the sand to
watch the day open up. This is the part of surfing her
mother doesn't understand. She thinks it's just about
people partying at the beach, goofing off and skipping
out on real life.

But to Rae it's also about being quiet and listening
to the world. Not just looking at nature, but feeling
your place in it. Knowing you're a part of Mother Nature's plans here.

And letting the ocean wash away all your worries.

Here, now, she can think only of what she loves. The new day, the water. Riding the waves, each one new, each one different.

Here, she's not a daughter or a math student or a big sister or a kid who's not sure what she wants to do with her life.

She's just a girl who surfs. A girl in the curl.

The sun begins to smile over Luna Bay, making the water sparkle like ginger ale, and Mother Nature whispers, *Come on in* . . .

Rae scrambles to her feet and picks up her board.

The water feels cold at first, then just cool and refreshing as she paddles out, bobbing through the shore break, headed for the swell just beyond the set of waves closest to the beach. She's planning to warm up here before she tries the bigger outside waves.

She reaches a swell and sits up on the board to survey the water. The tide is out. The waves are going to be steep. It feels perfect.

And then the waters are invaded by a school of sharks—loud raucous guys who come crashing in off the beach, showing off, crowding into her space, gawking, putting on a show. Riding the shore break right in front of her, when there are empty beaches as far as anyone can see in both directions.

Rae is really mad.

What show-offs. What jerks! she thinks. She hates guys who don't take girl surfers seriously. As if the sport belongs only to them, as if a woman's place is on the beach.

She floats on her board, waiting for them to get tired of this place, or bored, or something, until they move on. One of them rides a wave all the way in and then paddles back, sits up on his board, and grins at her. A bony, broken-nosed boy with stringy bleached hair. Proud of himself.

"Okay," Rae says. "How about a little impromptu contest?"

Surfer Dude squints at her. Finally he says, "What's a prom-too—don't I need a tux for that?"

Rae shakes her head. "*Impromptu*. Meaning 'unplanned.' 'Off the cuff.' Like, let's just do it, okay?"

Surfer Dude scowls. "I know what it means. I was making a joke, okay?"

Rae chuckles. "So how 'bout it?"

"What?"

"You against me—a little one-on-one?"

"Huh," he says dismissively. He looks back over his shoulder to check out what his buddies are doing.

Rae knows she should just ignore him. But something in the way he just blows her off really provokes her. She should let it go, but instead she calls out to him.

"What's the matter? Scared a *girl* might show you up?"

That gets his attention. "Like you could!" He fakes a laugh. It sounds like a bark. Now he's mad. "Get out of my way, little girl. I've got some real surfing to do."

"I have as much right to be here as you or anybody else," Rae shoots back.

He ignores her, then chases after the peak of the

next wave and climbs over it. She watches him disappear down the other side. She hates to admit it, but he's not half-bad.

She makes a move to take the next wave in the set, but one of Surfer Dude's friends cuts in front of her. He goes over the lip off balance and cartwheels. He surfaces a minute later, grounded on a sandbar.

Now Rae's the one wearing a grin.

"Hey, aren't you late for school?" he shouts.

"Yeah," the original Dude says, floating nearby. "You're missing show-and-tell!"

Laughter ripples through the lineup.

Rae's just about had enough. She looks for a wave. *I'll show-and-tell them*, she thinks. *They're the ones who ought to be in . . .*

School. Oh, yeah, Rae thinks. *As in—the place I was supposed to be—*

Rae glances at her dive watch, a present that her father gave her not long after he moved to Chicago.

In four and a half minutes!

She doesn't have time to be choosy. Rae grabs the next bus back to the beach, cringing at her less-than-graceful exit. She steadies her board and pulls off the leash, then jogs out of the water.

"Don't go away mad, just go away!" one of the boys cackles.

Her face burns. She feels like shouting something back. *But I don't have time to waste on little boys. I'm going to be late!*

2

School bells ring all over Crescent Cove High and the halls go from empty to instantly overflowing with students. The school day is over and everyone's making a fast escape. Lockers creak open and bang shut. All the exit doors are now propped wide open. In front of the school five girls with books in their arms hold a meeting.

Luna, Kanani, Isobel, Cricket, and Rae.

Rae explains why she was late for first period, blaming the boys who interrupted her morning set of waves.

Cricket shrugs. "Guys are kind of like jellyfish. A low form of life occasionally found in shallow water along the beach. Avoid contact." Cricket is always quick with the wisecracks. But it's hard to know what she's really thinking. Sometimes it seems as if Cricket is down on everyone of the male variety. She doesn't trust them much. After all, her dad—equal parts renowned surfer and elusive beach bum—walked out on her and her mom when she was little.

"Not all guys," says Luna, who has a very cool dad. And who's been in love before, even with two guys at once.

Isobel is braiding her beautiful long black hair. "Macho men—who needs them? It was the same back in Colorado. The cowboys think they own the slopes." She shrugs and tosses her thick braid over her shoulder. "Just forget about them."

"Forget about them?" Rae exclaims. She can't believe her friends aren't more upset. "I can't, you guys. It's losers like them who keep women down in this sport."

"Hey, don't let it get to you," Kanani soothes, slipping her arm around Rae's shoulders. "There's room in the world for all kinds."

Rae rolls her eyes. She can't believe her friends aren't more upset. Kanani she understands. She's the laid-back soul-surfer type, never caring much for competition, wanting instead to just commune with nature. Of all Rae's friends, Kanani is most into the sport's Hawaiian roots and its pursuit as an individual pastime for pleasure, health, and oneness with nature.

Rae definitely feels plugged into that side of it, too, but something in her wants to compete. When those guys invaded her space in the surf, it was like a challenge. Yeah, she was furious, but there was more to it—they represented competition.

"It does matter, Kanani," she insists. "It's just like a lot of the surfing magazines or books on the sport. You rarely see anything about a girl unless it's how she looks in a bikini in some ad."

"So read the girl surfing magazines," Isobel says.

"That's the point," Rae says. "There shouldn't have to be 'girl' surfing magazines."

"The big surfing magazines are never going to pay attention to us because they all follow the pro tour, which is mostly all-guy events," Cricket says. "Which reminds me. There's a women's event here in two weeks. Who's signing up with me?"

"Me, definitely," Luna says.

"I'm in, too," Rae says.

At home Rae's mom is in a weird mood. Even weirder than normal. Bad moods aren't unusual these days, ever since her dad moved to Chicago to take a job transfer. Rae still gets a sick feeling in the pit of her stomach whenever she remembers the sound of her parents fighting down the hall from her room.

The silverware drawer rattles as her mom yanks it open. "Can I get a little help in here, girls?"

Rae trades a look with her sister, Sherri. Sherri is twelve. She cried like a baby when her mother announced their parents were separating. She still believes their parents will get back together, once they've calmed down. She still believes everything will be like it used to be. Just like in some fairy tale or rerun on TV.

Rae secretly shared those feelings in the beginning, thought maybe her parents just needed some space. But her parents are so different in so many ways, and they seem to want such different things, that now she has her doubts. Maybe they would have a better chance if her dad were still here, where they could work on things.

But as the weeks and months go by, and Dad settles into a life in Chicago, it's hard for Rae not to shut the door on hope and try to get used to the here-and-now. It's less painful that way.

Rae helps Mom with some last-minute dinner prep while Sherri sets the table.

Maybe Mom's just tired from a hard day, Rae thinks.

But things aren't any better over dinner. No one argues or complains. No one does anything. There's no conversation.

Finally Rae asks, "Mom, what's wrong?"

"Don't talk with your mouth full," Mom replies, dodging the question.

"Sorry," Rae mumbles behind her hand and swallows, then stares into her plate.

Mom sighs then. "I'm sorry, girls. I don't mean to be so irritable. I . . ." Her hand flutters in the air like a wounded seagull. "I've just got a lot on my mind."

"It's okay, Mom," Sherri says softly, giving her mom a big smile.

Rae shakes her head at her sister. Sherri thinks that if everyone just smiles, everything will work out fine.

"Um, by the way." Mom stirs the straw in her glass of diet soda and stares at the cubes. "You guys each got a package today. From FedEx."

"We did?" Rae exclaims. She and her sister never get anything by FedEx. Luna's on a first-name basis with all the delivery guys. But Rae's mom is so not into shopping online. Doesn't trust it.

"Who's it from?" Sherri asks curiously.

Mom shrugs casually. "Your dad," she says nonchalantly, as if the packages were nothing short of junk mail.

Sherri's fork clatters to her plate.

Rae shoves back her chair. "Why didn't you *say* so?"

Rae hasn't heard from her dad in over a week! She jumps up from the table. Sherri's instantly at her side.

"Where is it?" they both gush.

Rae grabs Sherri's arm. "I wonder what he sent us?"

"I hope it's clothes!" Sherri exclaims.

"Clothes?" Rae shrieks, laughing. "You want to wear clothes *Dad* picked out?"

"Eww! You're right! Gross! So what do you think he sent?"

"I don't know! Maybe it's—"

"Girls!" Mom shouts.

Rae and her sister freeze, startled.

"Finish your dinner," Mom says through clenched teeth.

"Oh, Mom, come on!" Rae says. "Can't we just—"

Mom points at Rae's chair at the table. "Sit."

Rae sags back into her chair. *Woof!* she feels like replying, but she restrains herself. Her mom is a rules freak. When she and Sherri were little and used to fight over toys, her mom actually would put the toys in time-out. "Work it out or time it out," she always said.

Rae stares at the olive-drab peas on her plate. She puts a spoonful in her mouth. *They're cold. Why can't we have French fries every night like normal families?* she thinks. She looks over at Sherri, who appears as if she's going to barf.

But they eat it all anyway. They have to. Or Mom won't let them have their packages.

At last Mom says okay, enough, heads into her bedroom, and emerges a moment later carrying two FedEx boxes—a smaller one on top of a large one—in her strong, tanned arms. The girls follow her into the living room, crowding her, touching the boxes, wondering what's inside. She puts the boxes down on the coffee table.

"Wow!" Sherri gushes gleefully. "They're *huge!*" She reaches for the bigger one, then frowns. "Huh! This one's for you, Rae."

"Hey, don't worry," Rae reassures her. "You know what they say about good things coming in small packages."

Sherri's face lights up again. "You're right, they *do* say that, don't they!"

Mom leans against the doorway, watching without a word, curious, as wary as a cat on a windowsill watching a dog. Sherri opens her box.

"Oh, my gosh!" Sherri shouts. "Rae, look! It's a digital camera! Cool!"

Mom's mouth hangs open as Sherri tears open the rest of the package.

Rae's impressed. She can't wait to open hers.

She rips back the cardboard and looks inside.

No way. It can't be!

It is!

Dad sent her the latest model notebook computer! *And it's not even my birthday!* Rae thinks.

Her hands tremble as she unwinds the bubble wrap. She's wanted her own computer forever! She barely gets to use her mom's; Mom has rules about that because it's mostly for her business. Rae's mom just doesn't get that a notebook computer is considered a basic necessity these days.

"Now I can surf the Net as often as I surf Luna Bay!" Rae whoops.

Then it dawns on her. Not everyone in the room is happy right now.

"I can't believe it!" Mom exclaims. "How can he afford these expensive presents?"

She glares at Rae, who just shrugs helplessly. "Who cares? Mom—it's a laptop!"

"*I* care!" Mom shouts, choking back angry tears. "I'm handling everything here, trying to expand my business. And I'm still barely making ends meet," she exclaims, "even with what he sends us, and he's buying laptops!"

Rae knows they've never been what people would call rich, but she feels like they've always been okay. Until recently, anyway. Now her mom's gotten extra tight with money. She's come home with store-brand cereal and one-ply toilet paper. Rae's seen her spending hours clipping coupons out of the Sunday paper.

"Wait, there's a letter," Rae says, reaching into her box. She opens it and reads aloud:

"'Dear girls, I'm sorry I haven't called in a while, I've been really busy—'"

"Yeah, right," Mom interrupts. "Doing what?"

Rae decides it might be better to scan the letter silently and translate for Mom. "It says he's been putting in lots of long hours for some big project, and they've given him a bonus."

"Easy for him," Mom mutters. "He doesn't have to put in long hours here, cooking for a family, or cleaning house, or helping with homework, all while running a business single handed. . . ."

"So, uh, he says he decided to treat us." Rae scans the rest of the letter. "He says he hopes Sherri likes the camera. 'Sherri, send me some pictures!' And he says now he and I can e-mail and IM, instant message, 'after you teach the old man how!' He says to tell Mom that the computer is to help me with homework, too, that he's expecting to see lots of As on my next report card!"

Rae smiles up at Mom, whose eyes are like slits.

Rae looks back at the letter and reads, " 'The only rule is—' "

"Where does he get off," Mom says. "Making rules from thousands of miles away!"

Rae reads on. " 'You have to share it with Sherri.' "

Rae glances at her sister. "This is so cool!"

Except Sherri looks about as happy as Mom. She pouts and tosses her own present back into the box.

Rae can't tell if her sister is mad or about to cry. "What's wrong?"

Sherri turns to Mom. "How come Rae gets a whole computer—and I just got a dumb camera?"

"Sherri," Rae says, "it's not a dumb camera. It's really nice."

Sherri makes a gagging motion. "It's not exactly a computer!"

"Okay," Rae says, "but we're sharing the computer, remember?" She's getting irritated. She would have loved to have a digital camera when she was Sherri's age. "Anyway, you're not old enough to have a computer all by yourself—"

"Not old enough?" Sherri exclaims. "You know, I'm not a baby even though you, Mom, and everybody else treat me like one! Dad, too! Doesn't he know I'm *twelve*?"

"Of course he does!" Rae protests.

Sherri kicks the FedEx boxes and wrappings on the floor out of frustration.

"Okay, whatever," Rae says, picking up the computer and turning toward her room.

"*Hold it!*"

Rae and Sherri freeze and look at Mom, who's really steamed now—like a volcano about to erupt. Her face is red, and Rae can easily imagine smoke jetting from her ears.

"It's bad enough that your father sends you these expensive presents out of nowhere," she declares, "but I will not have you two squabbling over them like spoiled brats. Is that clear?"

"We're sorry, Mom," Rae says, giving Sherri the evil eye. "Right, Sherri?"

Sherri folds her arms and looks the other way.

Rae figures she's done her part at least and starts to leave again.

"*Come back here, young lady!*"

"Mom, what is it?" Rae says, impatient. "I said I was sorry. I even said I was sorry for *both* of us!"

"No computer until the table is cleared and the dishwasher is loaded."

Rae groans. "But, Mom, I want to go set this up so I can e-mail Dad and thank him—"

"Dirty dishes now, fabulous toys later." Mom stands her ground. Rae and Sherri head into the kitchen.

When Mom leaves for the barn to check on the horses, Rae can hear her all the way outside, complaining. "Where does he get off. . . . He's just trying to buy their affection."

Rae throws herself into clearing the table, scraping

the dishes, loading the dishwasher. She wants out of there ASAP so she can get to her computer.

Sherri is just the opposite. With a dishrag dangling from one hand, she picks up a single fork and slowly, slowly walks it over to the dishwasher. Then she shuffles back to the table and picks up a spoon.

"Hey, come on!" Rae complains.

Sherri turns and gives Rae a totally innocent look. "What?"

"You know what. You're barely helping!"

"Well," Sherri says with a fake smile, "I'm just your *baby* sister. Maybe it's the best I can do. Maybe I'll do better when I'm *old enough*!"

And with that, she throws the dishrag down on the floor and storms off to her room.

"I'm gonna tell Mom!" Rae hollers after her, but Sherri just slams her door.

Rae winces, but lets her go. Of course she's not going to run and tell Mom—it'll just make things worse. So Rae turns back to finish up herself. It'll be much easier without Sherri in the way.

And what's Sherri's problem, anyway?

Rae fills the dishwasher with detergent, turns on the machine, then hurries to her room to set up her laptop.

I'm not going to let Mom or Sherri make me feel guilty, she thinks.

Really.

I'm not.

I wish Dad were here, Rae thinks as she struggles to set up her computer.

At last she does what she should have done in the first place: she calls Cricket.

"SOS, girlfriend!" she says when Cricket picks up.

"What's up? Are you okay?"

"I'm great but stranded," Rae says. "My dad just sent me a laptop, but I'm having some trouble setting it up. Can you come over?"

"I'm on my way."

Fifteen minutes later Cricket arrives with a bag of chips, a two-liter bottle of soda, and great advice.

"This is so cool," Cricket says as she goes to work. "And, like, your dad just sent it out of the blue?" She shakes her head. "Lucky girl."

"Yeah," Rae says. "Except Mom had a major fit about it."

"Well, I guess she doesn't like him giving you presents when she's the one stuck giving you chores."

Rae grins at her friend. "Your wisdom amazes me, O Great One."

Cricket shrugs and turns her attention back to the computer. Growing up with a single working mom has made her unusually self-sufficient. Building and fixing things without help is just normal for Cricket.

"This is a new computer but it was probably used in the store as a demo, with some kind of ad running on it. I'll bet your dad got a little better price on this than one wrapped up in the box. There's nothing wrong with that, you just have to run these recovery disks to wipe the hard drive back to Day One."

Soon the laptop is up and running. Cricket gives Rae some final instructions on how to install more software. Then she heads for the door. "I've gotta split. Mom's working late, and I want to be there when she gets home from work."

"Thanks," Rae says. "You want your chips?"

"They're yours. There's plenty more where they came from back at the house." She gives Rae a thumbs-up. "Hey, e-mail me, okay? And call me if you have any trouble with the laptop."

Rae digs out another chip. "Thanks, I owe you one. Or two."

Cricket leaves. Rae goes online and sets up an e-mail account. Then she e-mails Cricket a quick thanks, and writes to her dad.

Dad—
Wow! Thanks, thanks, thanks! I can't believe you
sent me a laptop! It's perfect. I love it! I'm sorry
you've been working so hard. We really miss you.
Sherri loves her camera

Rae pauses. Okay, so she's stretching the truth a little. *But Sherri will love her camera—as soon as she stops
pouting! Rae thinks. What else should I tell him?*
She thinks of her mom and suddenly Rae has an
overwhelming need to tell Dad everything and talk
about the separation. She longs to tell him how she's
feeling, and how hard it is on Sherri—how hard it is
on Mom, too.
Her hands hover over the keys . . .
But she can't make the words come out right.
Maybe later, when they're IM'ing, she'll be able to tell
him how she feels. So for now, she just keeps it happy.

Let's make a date to IM soon. It's really easy—
you'll love it. When's a good time for you?
Thanks again, Dad. I love you!
Rae

Next she sends a group e-mail to her friends to let
them know she's wired.
Luna's online, so Rae sends her an instant message.

RAE: Luna, it's me. Rae.

LUNA: cool! just got your e-mail. now we can talk whenever!

RAE: :) RU signed up for the Jam?

LUNA: yes. what about u? better hurry. it's first come first serve. go 2 their web site.

RAE: OK. BTW U shoulda seen Mom. Totally ballistic!

LUNA: y

RAE: The computer. She's freaked out, thinks Dad's trying to buy our affection, that kind of thing. Like, what am I supposed to do? Send it back?

RAE: u still there?

Rae clicks on the button that sends the message she typed earlier.

RAE: sorry

LUNA: got it. i wish id gone 2 the beach w/u this morning. wanna meet 2morrow???

RAE: 6?

LUNA: k

RAE: bye

Then Rae types in the website for the Seventh Street competition. *This is so cool!* she thinks. It's lucky she can register this way. The deadline's the next day. She completes a registration and clicks DONE. Somewhere on the Internet a computer sends an automatic reply to her mailbox. She's in. All she has to do is bring her tournament résumé credentials and a board, of course. Rae e-mails the news to all of her friends.

Rae glances at the clock on her screen. *Whoa! I've been on over an hour,* she realizes. She hasn't heard a peep out of Sherri and starts to feel guilty. So she goes to Sherri's room and taps on the door.

There's no answer. Rae can hear the pulsing beat of some rap song playing and guesses Sherri can't hear her. She tries the door, but it's locked. So she knocks louder. "Hey, Sherri, it's me! I've got the laptop set up. Want to try it out?"

Still no response, so she pounds on the door. "Come on, Sherri. Open up. You can send Dad an e-mail."

"Go away! I'm busy!" Sherri finally shouts through the door.

Rae frowns. "Fine! Have it your way!" She waits a minute to see if Sherri changes her mind, then gives up and heads back to her room.

She gets this kind of sick feeling in her stomach. When their mom and dad started fighting, Rae and Sherri got closer, in a way. At times it felt like the whole world was divided up into two sides. The kids versus the grown-ups.

I hate what this has done to us, Rae thinks.

Not that Sherri was totally blameless. "It's not *my*

fault Dad sent me a laptop," Rae mutters to herself. "And I'm *trying* to share it. If I had a big sister offering me time on her computer, I'd jump on it! You wouldn't see me locking myself up in my room. I'd be online!"

Rae stops and looks in the mirror. The way she's talking reminds her of Mom.

Rae shrugs and sits down at the computer to do a little surfing on surfing. This is so cool! All she has to do is type in a word or two, and the computer transports her to all kinds of places. It's like a magic-carpet ride all around the world. There's even a surfing Web site in Japanese!

It doesn't seem like she's been on all that long when her mom sticks her head in the doorway. "Did you study for your math test?"

Math test! Rae forgot all about it! She glances at the clock. She can't believe how long she's been online! Quickly she signs off and grabs her book. "I'm up for it, Mom," she says. "But I guess it wouldn't hurt to review it one more time before I go to sleep."

Mom gives her a penetrating look, then scowls at the computer. "Okay. But lights out in twenty minutes."

"Gotcha." Rae grins till her mom leaves—then digs in her desk drawer for her flashlight. She's barely looked at her math book. She's going to be doing some serious studying under the covers tonight!

4

*R*ae's heart is pounding: she's riding a freaking *monster* wave, like nothing she's ever seen in Luna Bay. And she's all alone. There's a strong angry wind, and it shoves her up the face of the wave, till she's grabbing air and the bottom seems to fall out of the world. Danger pumps her veins full of adrenaline as she stares down into the jaws of a drop that's taller than her high school. And gravity wants her.

Suddenly she's invaded by surfboards painted like sharks, guys cutting in on her, only . . .

Something is wrong, they're *not* guys, they're *numbers*—like seven, one, nine—all lined up like an algebra equation, and they taunt her as she plunges into the suds, tumbling like a hoodie in the washing machine. . . .

The number boys are her first clue—she's been dreaming, and now she's coming up for air. The sec-

24

ond clue is that she's drooling facedown on something hard. She cracks one eye. *Math book. Must have fallen asleep studying . . .*

She reaches to turn off the light shining in her face, then realizes it's not her lamp. It's the sun.

Unless it's Saturday, it should still be dark. She scrambles out of bed to check the time on her computer screen, which she's left online all night. God, she's late! But she sees she's got mail, and she thinks, *Dad!*

Eagerly she clicks open her mailbox. But there's nothing from her dad yet. Only some saved messages from her buds and some spam labeled "Refinance your mortgage now!"

She deletes it, dances in and out of the shower, heads to the kitchen with a mouth full of toothpaste and her backpack slung over one shoulder.

The kitchen's deserted, and Rae remembers her mom had an early beach ride scheduled with an AARP breakfast club. Sherri must have already caught her ride to school.

Mom, in an efficient message of love and health news, has left out a bowl, a spoon, and some store-brand bran cereal along with a glass of calcium-fortified orange juice. Rae shudders, drinks the juice, but ignores the bran and the lavender Post-it note stuck to the box. *More chores*, she thinks. But she doesn't have time for chores or for breakfast. She grabs a Power Bar from the cabinet and shoves out the door.

She makes it to school two minutes before the bell

rings and jogs to the front entrance, where she sees Luna waiting with a tall paper cup. "Where were you?" she asks.

"Overslept," Rae says. "Too much surfing. The computer kind."

Luna grins. "I brought you a mocha anyway. I'm not sure how hot it is anymore."

But Rae gratefully accepts it, tears off the lid, and downs a huge, lukewarm slug as they hurry inside. "Thanks, I really need this. I've got a major math test first period."

"Mr. Levinson?"

Rae nods.

"Ouch."

"Tell me about it." Rae reaches her locker and spins the combination lock. "Mom's been watching my grades like a hawk lately. It's like she's making up for Dad being gone by being twice as tough."

"Mmm," Luna says, nodding sympathetically, but Rae can tell her friend doesn't know what else to say. Luna's parents are perfect lovebirds and Luna gets along great with both of them. How could she possibly understand what it's like?

In homeroom Rae hides behind Jim Faber's massive football shoulders during announcements and stares at her math book. She knows last-minute cramming just doesn't cut it in algebra, but maybe she can absorb some final vibes from the page that will help her get through the test.

She feels a tug on the back of her shirt and whirls around.

Jeff Jamison snickers. "What have you been up to?" To her blank look, he whispers loudly, "Your shirt's on inside out!"

"Hey, it's the new look," she whispers back. But as soon as homeroom is over, she heads into the girls' room to change her shirt.

Her math class is on the other side of the school, and the last vibrations of the late bell are fading away as she slides into class and sinks into her seat at the back of the room.

Mr. Levinson shoots her a look, but merely says, "Morning, class. I hope you're all ready for the big test." A smile tugs at his lips. "It's *wicked*."

Rae groans along with the rest of the class as Mr. Levinson walks to the front of the room, handing out stacks of tests to pass back on each row. "Please put away all books and backpacks . . ."

Two seats ahead of her across the aisle, Isobel turns around, eyebrows raised. "You okay?" she whispers.

Rae rolls her eyes and shrugs.

"All eyes front . . ." Mr. Levinson says.

Isobel gives Rae a thumbs-up and turns around. Rae takes her test from the kid in front of her and groans. The thing is three pages long!

She can feel the adrenaline kick in—the fight-or-flight syndrome, her science teacher calls it—as everyone tucks in for the race against the clock.

Okay, no biggie, Rae tries to tell herself. *Think of it as a sports event. It's just like that monster wave in your dream. Focus. Psych yourself up. Then jump on the board and shoot the curl!*

Almost an hour later Rae is suffering a major wipe-out. She's working problems halfway, skipping some to go on to the next one, trying to save the worst ones for last. Unfortunately, they're all the worst. *How could I have gotten so far behind in this class?* she wonders. It's not her best subject, but she's always done okay. She feels as if she's never even seen some of this stuff.

Don't panic, she tells herself. And then she begins to hear unmistakable sounds: papers rustling, people stretching in their seats, feet shuffling. Her classmates are finishing the test.

Okay, now you can panic!

Ahead of her, Isobel gets up and turns in her paper. She's always the first one finished, an unbelievable math magician. *Maybe I should have studied with her,* Rae thinks forlornly. Her friend glances back and mouths, *Good luck!*

Rae waves, then stares back at her paper. The numbers line up and taunt her like those rowdy surf boys who ruined her day at the beach. Even magic couldn't help her now.

Soon other smart kids start getting up. Then even the regular kids are leaving! *How can they?* Rae thinks. *I've got half a dozen problems left!*

And then the shadow of doom falls across her paper. Mr. Levinson, looming over her, silently waiting. Rae glances up and realizes . . . *I'm the last student left in the room!*

She rushes to finish the problem she's on, writing down things she knows don't make sense, then frantically erases—and tears a pitiful little hole in the paper.

Mr. Levinson lays a gentle but firm hand on her shoulder. "Time's up, Rae."

Sighing, Rae nods and hands over her paper. Then she grabs her backpack and flees. *Gotta get out of here before Mr. Levinson glances at my test and shrieks in horror!*

Rae weaves her way through the crowds to her next class, her head down, not in the mood for her normal meet-and-greet. Her mom's really been on her case about her grades lately, worried she'll become a "surf bum" instead of doing the "sensible thing" and going to college. Rae's always been a pretty good student, but now her mom is talking about visiting colleges, and worrying about grades and SATs and things like scholarships and college loans.

But Rae doesn't need to wait for her grades to know how she did on this test.

Looks like I just handed Mom a good reason to ban me from surfing for life!

5

*R*ae's with her friends. They're on their way to the beach. Rae should be happy.

But she's not.

She's worrying about her math test. And the fight she had with her mom. And Sherri.

"I need some time in the water," she tells Luna as they take the beach access from the parking lot. "Just to stay sane."

But it's not going to be that easy. Before any of them even see the water they hear the sound of boys. Lots of them. They've taken over the beach.

Rae scans the lineup and groans. "Oh, great. Look who's here."

Luna shades her eyes. "Who?"

"Those guys from yesterday," Rae says. "The ones from the 'No Girls Allowed' club."

"So, who cares," Isobel says, waxing her board.

"There's room for everybody." She jabs Rae. "Especially when they look like that blond guy."

"Hello!" Rae exclaims. "Who are you and what are you on, 'cause I know you did not just go there."

"Not the skinny one with the big nose," Isobel clarifies. "The other one. Anyway, I just got here." She winks at Rae. "And I think I need a closer look at these 'losers.'" She picks up her board and jogs toward the water.

Reluctantly Rae follows the others to the waves.

Surfer Dude has spotted her. "Hey, guys, look," he shouts. "Kindergarten just let out!"

"Very funny," Rae hollers back.

"Hey, just ignore them," Kanani says.

Rae tries. The girls paddle out, and when a boy surfs in, a girl assumes his old position on the other side of the wave. They get their turns.

Rae slips in when Surfer Dude leaves. His ride ends in the shallow water, where he stops and stands with one arm cocked on his hip, showing her that he's getting a little impatient.

He's waiting to observe Rae's ride.

Well, okay.

So when is she going to take off? Ever?

When I'm ready.

Rae's used to being judged. She loves it, in a way. She's won her share of amateur contests up and down the beach. What's different in this case is the attitude. In a competition, the crowds, and most of the other surfers, are basically on your side. Everyone wants to see a good ride. Here, Rae's being watched by someone who would like nothing better than to see a total wipeout.

Which isn't going to happen.

She picks a wave, makes her move, and spills off the peak. It's not a big one, but that's another kind of challenge, looking good on a mushy wave. She needs to get the most out of it. She carves up and down the wall, feeling good. She rides it all the way out, finishes with a confident jump off the board into the water. She makes it look as easy as someone entering a swimming pool.

"Oh! That was so AWESOME!" Surfer Dude mocks. "Can I have your autograph?"

Rae frowns. There is something she'd like to give him: a punch in the nose. The nose that somebody else already broke, once. Which doesn't surprise her. *Why am I letting this jerk get to me?* she thinks at last.

There's a reason. It's not just him. It's him and all the guy surfers just like him who think girls can't—or shouldn't—surf.

"Listen, don't you pigeons have some sunbathing to do?"

Rae ignores him.

"Why don't you go park your little bikini bottoms on a beach towel—and give the real surfers some space out here to work?"

No reaction.

"This sucks, man," Surfer Dude says, frustrated. Kanani's strategy, ignoring them, is working. "Let's blow this popsicle stand and find some like, real waves somewhere else, already. Okay?"

Rae laughs. She can't help it. "Don't you love the way he talks? Is he like, 'gettin' a Dell, dude?' "

Luna howls. "I love it! And now we have the beach to ourselves."

Rae decides she has enough hassles in her life right now. She doesn't need to find new things to think about, to make her even more upset and miserable. It's time to do a little soul-surfing with her friends.

Then she spots a familiar figure on the beach, waving at her.

"Hey, Rae," Luna says. "That's your mom."

Rae gets a funny feeling in her stomach. Her mom looks really upset. She hopes nothing's wrong. Oh, my gosh! Rae hasn't heard back from her father. *What if something's happened to Dad? Or to Sherri?*

Rae's too worried to surf her way in. Lying down on her board, she paddles in to the next wave and holds on while it delivers her express to the shore.

When the water spends itself in the shallow water, she releases her leash and jogs up to her mother. "Mom! Is everything okay?"

"No, everything is not okay," her mom says. Now Rae can see that she looks more angry than upset. "Didn't you see my note this morning?"

"Um . . . the purple Post-it on the cereal box?"

"Yes. Well—did you *read* it?"

"Well, not exactly," Rae hedges. "I was kind of in a hurry."

Mom rolls her eyes, exasperated. "It was a reminder that you were supposed to pick up Sherri from her friend Elena's house after school and take her to tap dance class for me this afternoon. Rae, we talked about this over the weekend."

Rae winces. "Sorry, Mom. I guess I forgot. I had kind of a hard day."

"Yeah, tell me about it," her mom mutters, running a hand through her hair. Then she sighs and forces a tired smile. "Okay, well, let's just go from here. I've got a group of riders showing up any minute at the stables. Can you take over? I need you to get Sherri to tap, hang around, and bring her home after class."

Rae wants nothing more than to head back to the water. But she just smiles and says, "Sure, no problem." Rae gazes at her mother's face. There are shadows beneath her eyes, and tired lines Rae never noticed before. Impulsively she throws her arms around her mom and gives her a quick hug.

"Rae!" her mom exclaims, jumping back.

Rae sees that she's left a wet imprint of herself on her mother's clothes. "Sorry."

Her mom sighs, but gives her a crooked smile. "S'okay. It'll dry. And . . . thanks for the hug. I really needed that."

Rae wants her mom to say more. She wants answers to questions she doesn't even know how to ask her.

A car horn honks loudly and long, and Rae glances up at the parking area. She sees her sister poke her head out of the car. "I'm gonna be late!" Sherri hollers.

Rae pulls on a T-shirt, throws her shorts into the backseat, and sits down on the driver's side on a beach towel. She drops her mom off at the stables, then heads to the dance school.

"Sorry about the mix-up," Rae tells her sister.

But Sherri is busy pouting with her head turned toward the window, so Rae just turns on the radio. She doesn't even argue when Sherri hits the scan button looking for a different station.

Soon Rae pulls into the drop-off lane at the front door of the dance school. "Okay. I'll pick you up in a—"

Slam! Sherri jumps out of the car and flounces through the door without a backward glance.

"You're welcome," Rae mutters as she drives off. The school is in a shopping center. Rae knows about a coffee shop a few doors down where she can wait. She parks, grabs her purse and her math book, goes inside, orders an iced decaf and a turtle brownie, and sits down at an outside table off by itself. Then she opens the math book.

She tries to look at her homework, really she does. For four whole minutes she concentrates on copying problems onto a sheet of notebook paper. But it happens to be one of those gorgeous people-watching days. The sunlight shines bright against a paint-box-blue sky; the ocean breeze ruffles the pages of her math book and teases her by sending her list of problems flying out across the sidewalk like a paper airplane.

Rae dashes after her homework, but as she leans down to snatch it from the gutter, she's suddenly attacked by a barking dog who knocks her onto her bottom and drenches her face with dog slobber.

"Barney!"

Even more wonderful is the human attached to the other end of his leash.

Drew!

"Sorry, Rae!" He pulls Barney off. All of a sudden, it's another perfect day.

Drew is a lifeguard. Rae met him several months ago when they ran into each other on the beach. That's when he discovered that she and her girlfriends had been taking care of his lost dog. Rae wouldn't call Drew her boyfriend, exactly, but they've gone out several times, and she wouldn't mind if their friendship grew into something more.

Barney settles down, Drew takes a seat, they hang out, talk surfing, and Rae forgets all about her math book.

And Sherri.

"Drew, what time is it?" Rae says, alarmed, astonished at how much time has passed without her realizing it.

She's supposed to pick up her sister. Class is way over. Rae can feel the daggers all the way over here.

Rae grabs her backpack and scribbles her new screen name on a napkin. "I just got a new computer," she tells Drew. "E-mail me!" Then she jogs to her car and pulls around to the dance school.

She can see Sherri in the window. One glance at her body language tells Rae all she needs to know about her mood.

Rae pulls up to the curb and tries a friendly wave. Scowling, Sherri jumps in the car. "Where *were* you?" she demands.

"Sorry," Rae says. To be honest, she remembers how not fun it is to be the kid standing alone, the last one picked up. "I was, uh, working on my math homework." She tries for humor. "You know how time flies when you're having fun!"

"Wait till I tell Mom!"

"What! Oh, come on, Sherri," Rae answers. "It was just a couple of minutes—"

"Seven*teen*," Sherri points out. "Maybe she'll ground you." She folds her arms and smirks. "Maybe she'll take your *computer* away!"

"Hey, no fair!"

"Yeah, well, life's not fair," Sherri gripes. "Haven't you learned that by now?"

Rae can't help herself. "Yeah, I have!" she shoots back. "You're not the only one whose life *sucks* right now, you know?"

Sherri's lower lip trembles, and she turns away to stare out the window without another word.

Here we go again, Rae thinks. This is not how she wanted things to turn out. She and Sherri need each other, now more than ever. "Hey," she says, and lays a hand on her sister's arm.

But Sherri jerks away, and the moment passes.

Rae drives the rest of the way home in silence.

As soon as they pull into the driveway, Sherri jumps out of the car and runs to the barn. Rae heads for the kitchen to start a salad for dinner, hoping to get on her mom's good side. She pulls out lettuce, peppers, tomatoes, starts to skip the broccoli, then changes her mind, going for extra brownie points.

Maybe her sister won't rat on her. *What good does it do Sherri to get Mom mad?* Rae thinks. But as soon as her mom comes in the door, it's clear. Sherri blabbed.

Mom gives her a lecture about paying attention to what's important, but surprisingly, only a short one. She looks tired, Sherri looks insulted that her tattling didn't get better results, and dinner passes with little conversation.

Rae hates it. She wants to ask her mom about her afternoon, tell Sherri a joke she heard at school.

How did things get so messed up? she wonders. It's almost like they've all been trying to continue living as if everything were okay, with Dad leaving. And now, suddenly, everyone's tired of pretending.

She should say something. Apologize. Debate. Yell—*something* to get it all out in the open.

But instead she just moves her broccoli florets from one side of the plate to the other.

After dinner Rae heads to her room to study, but soon it's time to go online for her IM "date" with her dad.

I could really stand to talk to somebody in my family who's still talking to me, she thinks.

She checks her buddy list, but he's not on yet. So she decides to send him an e-mail.

Maybe if I tell him what it's like here, how much we miss him. . . .

Her hands hover over the keys, and it's déjà vu all over again.

Instead she types:

I'M HERE, DAD. WHERE ARE U?

6

*R*ae tries in vain to go online and find out if her application was accepted, but the Web site is down.

It's probably posted at City Center, she thinks. All the town offices are there, including the parks department, which runs the beaches. All the surfing contest schedules and bulletins are posted there.

"Mom, I have to go downtown," Rae calls, halfway out the door. "I have to find out if I made the cut for this surfing contest." She doesn't even wait for an answer. She's got to go.

City Center is mobbed. There are lines of people waiting to find out about the competition. Rae's whole gang is there: Luna, Kanani, Cricket, Isobel.

"What's the problem?" Rae asks.

"The network is down," Cricket says. "The only thing they have running is that one desktop." She points down the line at a harried-looking woman peering intently at a monitor, listening to the person at the front of the line and typing furiously.

"The bad vibrations here are so intense," Luna says with a shudder.

Rae hears a familiar voice coming from behind. Bad vibrations? What a coincidence. It's Surfer Dude.

"Hey, I didn't know the tournament had a children's division," he says.

"Well, Chaz, obviously they do," one of his buddies says, with an exaggerated nod of the head toward the girls.

"How clever they are," Rae says, rolling her eyes.

Cricket shakes her head sadly. "It is a shame," she says.

"What?" Kanani asks.

"Chaz. He has such great hair. And nothing to show for it underneath."

Rae and her friends crack up.

"At least we don't have to surf with them," Isobel says. "I hate to surf with egomaniacs. It's so hard to hear the pounding of the waves over all their bragging."

The line moves up a step.

Then another.

Then another.

Finally, after thirty minutes, Rae and the gang are at the front.

And the registrar says to Rae, "Sorry, we don't have an application for you."

"What?" Rae is dumbfounded. "Are you sure? I applied online."

The woman shrugs. "Modem problems."

Rae can't believe this. "I got a reply e-mail confirming my application."

"Well, that's different," the woman says. "You have a confirmation number, then. What is it?" She looks at Rae, ready to type it in.

"I don't know," Rae admits.

"You didn't print it out?" the woman says. She seems irritated.

I'm the one who should be mad, Rae thinks.

"No, I didn't," Rae says. "I got the e-mail on my laptop. I don't walk around with a printer hooked up to my laptop."

The woman shrugs. "Sorry. I know it's disappointing, but there's nothing I can do. There are only twenty-four slots open in this competition anyway. Twelve in Division A and twelve in Division B. Lots of people don't get accepted." She nods her head at the long line of hopefuls behind Rae.

"I know that," Rae says. "I mean, I know you have to qualify. I put all my contest wins on my application. I just want to know definitely if I got accepted or rejected."

The woman sighs heavily and types Rae's name in again, then shakes her head. "Well, I can see who's in Division B and you're not in there."

Then she frowns. "Wait a minute," she says, and types something more. "There you are."

Rae looks at the monitor. It says "RAY PERRAULT."

"Somebody fixed the way you spelled your name," the woman tells her. "Fixed it wrong, that is. Anyway, the good news is, you're in."

"I thought you said I wasn't."

"You weren't. In Division B, that is. You most definitely are in Division A. The men's."

"But I'm a girl," Rae says.

"Not according to this," the woman says. "Ray."

Kanani giggles.

"Oh my God." Luna gasps.

Rae blushes. She wishes the woman wouldn't talk so loud. Other people are looking now. Not only that, Chaz and his buddies have chosen that exact moment to catch up in the line next to them. Another guy explains the situation to Chaz.

"They signed her up for Division A. Thought her name was R-A-Y."

The registrar looks unhappy. "The real problem is I can't put you in Division B because all the places are taken."

Chaz pouts. "Now that is a shame!"

"And I can't put you in Division A because that's the men's."

"Aw!" Chaz says.

Rae squints at him, then turns back to the woman. "Just a minute. You can't just kick me out. You've already accepted my application. I'm in Division A. You said so."

The woman laughs nervously. No one else does.

Chaz smirks. "Yeah, right."

Rae smiles at him and shrugs. "I'm in, Chaz. There's nothing you can do about it. Or her. Or anybody."

"No way!" Chaz shouts.

"What's the problem?" Rae says. Her friends gather around her.

"Yeah, what's the problem?" says Cricket.

"Give me a break," Chaz pleads to the surfers standing around, looking for support. "You can't put a girl in the guys' division."

Rae turns back to the woman. "I'd like my beach badge, please. Rae Perrault, contestant, Division A."

At first the woman refuses. She calls a supervisor over and they have a meeting. The supervisor, a man in dark glasses, tries one more time.

"Try to understand, miss," he says.

"Is it in the rules?" Rae asks.

"Of course it is." But he sounds nervous.

"Okay," Rae says. It's a long shot, but she's a good bluffer. "Can you show me where it states in the rules that I have to be male to compete in Division A?"

The officials leaf through the rules.

"Actually," the woman says, with a half-smile on her face, "it doesn't say. Technically, I guess it doesn't matter. You qualified, and you *were* accepted." She looks at her boss.

"Well," he says with a shrug, "yeah, I guess you do have a point . . . and a valid one."

Rae pumps the air with her fist and cheers, along

with her friends. A crowd has gathered now, with people debating the issue.

Chaz bumps into her as he and his buddies leave.

"This is stupid," he says angrily. "You have no right to surf with the guys."

"What's the matter?" Rae responds. "Scared a girl might beat you?"

Chaz's face turns red as he shoves past her. "You stole somebody else's place, girl," he says. "You messed up."

Rae looks back at the crowd.

Guys and girls are arguing about it.

She wonders if she's making a mistake.

7

"**R**ae, wake up," her mom says the next morning. "You've got a phone call."

"Say I'll call them back," she mumbles into her pillow.

Her mom pulls the covers back. "I think you should take the call."

Rae rolls over and takes the cordless phone. " 'Lo?"

A guy is talking. Rae tries to listen. It sounds like he says . . . how does she feel about . . . *breaking something*?

Huh? Rae sits up and rubs her eyes. "Sorry, I just woke up. What did you say I broke? Am I in trouble?"

"Oh, sorry about that." He chuckles. "And no, you're not in trouble at all. It's just, I'd like to interview you for the paper."

"Me? Why?"

"I got a call that you're competing in the Seventh Street Showdown. What I said was 'How does it feel to be breaking down barriers like this in sports?' "

Rae's mom is making all kinds of signals at her. Like, *Who is it?* And pointing at her watch.

Finally Rae pulls herself together and manages to thank the guy for his interest, but could he call her after school?

"Well, I have a deadline. Can I just ask you what made you decide to—"

Rae is flattered, but there's no way she's going to be interviewed by a reporter while she's still in her pajamas. Her mind's as tangled as her hair this early in the morning!

"Oh! Excuse me!" Rae interrupts politely. "I think I hear the school bus. I've really got to run!"

As soon as she hangs up, the phone rings again. Rae hands the phone to her mom and heads into the bathroom to brush her teeth.

A moment later her mom has followed her to give her the phone back. "It's for you, again."

"Is it Dad?"

Mom shakes her head.

Rae takes the phone, her mouth still full of toothpaste. "Huh-mo?"

It's another reporter. She's heard about Rae entering the guys' competition. "I just wanted to ask you—"

"How about after school?" Rae suggests. "I'm usually at the beach in the afternoons. Maybe you can catch me there."

"Where do you go to school?" the reporter asks.

"Crescent Cove High," Rae answers. "But really, I've

got to go. My mom has to drive me to school, and she'll be late to work if I don't leave now. Bye!"

Rae clicks off and hands the phone to her mom, who is looking at her as if she's just dyed her hair green. "Persistent telemarketer?" she asks dryly.

Rae shakes her head. "Something like that." She dresses for school, then joins her family at the kitchen table. She's digging into some cereal that actually has some bright fruity colors for a change when she feels her mom and sister staring at her. She glances up.

"Well?" Mom says. "What was that all about?"

Rae shrugs. "Oh, I signed up for this tournament. I told you I had to go down to the City Center, remember? Their Web site was down. Anyway, they accidentally registered me in the men's competition. You know, because of the Rae thing? They thought I was a guy." She grins at Sherri. "Isn't that funny?"

Mom sips her coffee. "So why do these reporters want to do a story on a clerical error?"

"Not exactly. At first they wanted to kick me out. I said it wasn't my mistake and they couldn't eliminate me. They checked the rule book, and it turned out I was right." Rae grins. "I'm going to surf against the guys! Isn't that cool?"

"What?" her mom exclaims. "When? Where?"

Rae realizes that in all the craziness going on at home, she forgot to mention that she'd signed up for the competition in the first place. "I guess I forgot to tell you about it. It's just a local competition, Mom. It's next Saturday and Sunday." She gulps down her juice. "It's going to be awesome!"

But her mom looks concerned. "Surfing against *boys*?" She shakes her head. "I don't know, Rae. Surfing's dangerous enough as it is, and you're so . . ."

Her mom doesn't finish the sentence, but she doesn't have to. And Rae can't help being touchy about it. "Short?" she says, annoyed. "Little? A shrimp?"

"I was going to say *petite,*" her mom says emphatically. "What's wrong with that? I think you're perfect just the way you are. But if you surf in the male competition, you'll be surfing against guys who are a whole lot bigger and *rougher* than you are—"

"Mom! Surfing is *not* a contact sport," Rae interrupts with a laugh. "It's not football! I don't have to knock them down. I just have to outsurf them."

Sherri isn't saying anything; she just stares at Rae over her presweetened cereal.

But Mom shakes her head. "In competition, people tend to take more, and bigger, risks. You could get hit with a board, too."

"Mom, I'll be fine," Rae assures her as she takes her dishes to the dishwasher. "Really. It's not a big deal."

Or maybe it is, Rae thinks later that day in math class.

Somehow everybody at school seems to have heard

about the competition. People she doesn't even know that well come up to her to ask her questions. Things like, *"Will they give you some kind of handicap because you're a girl?"* Or, *"What if you meet some hunk you want to go out with? Are you still going to try to beat him?"*

For once, she's actually glad to escape into math class, to get away from all the attention. Rae's not shy, but she's never been the kind of girl who thrives—or even cares—about being in the spotlight. She could have gone out for the spring musical if she wanted to get stared at.

"All right, class," Mr. Levinson says, holding up a sheaf of papers. "I've got your tests to hand back. And I must say I was quite impressed," he adds wryly, "with the *creativity* of some of your answers. . . ."

Rae groans. Even from the back row, she can see a lot of red marks on most of the papers. The kid in front of her hands her test over her shoulder. Rae closes her eyes, afraid to look.

Just then the door to the classroom opens. Rae looks up in surprise. A nicely dressed woman with a stiff, blond-highlighted hairdo enters, followed by a guy in jeans carrying a camcorder with an intensely bright light attached on top shining straight ahead. "Excuse me," the woman says to no one in particular. "Can you tell me where I can find Rae Perrault?"

Rae freezes as the whole planet seems to turn its gaze upon her. The woman takes her cue from the class and locks eyes with Rae instantly. "Hi, I'm Heather Bancroft, Channel Seven Eyewitness News.

I'd like to ask you some questions about the upcoming Seventh Street event."

Rae's mouth is hanging open. "Uh . . ."

Heather turns to her cameraman. "Hey, Chuck," she mutters out of the side of her mouth, "be sure to get some shots of the teacher, the blackboard, the other students. . . ." Then she tries to make her way past Mr. Levinson to get closer to Rae, and Chuck follows suit.

Then some of Rae's classmates start to crowd around her, goofing off, trying to get on TV, the way people do in Times Square on New Year's Eve. Isobel is trying to squeeze through to be with her.

"I'm sorry," Mr. Levinson is saying. "I'm afraid you can't—"

But his voice is drowned out by the commotion.

Rae is *so* not prepared for this. She quickly sinks down in her seat, hoping her fierce blush will look more like a sunburn on TV.

Before she can say anything, she hears her principal coming in the door. "Excuse me, *excuse me*—"

The kids part like the Red Sea. Principal Harding is built like a truck, can bench-press a school bus, and looks a little like Arnold Schwarzenegger.

"I'm sorry," he booms politely as he nearly lifts the cameraman off his feet. "All visitors are required to sign in at the office."

Heather Bancroft protests as she follows them out. "But sir, if Ms. Perrault could just answer a few questions—"

As soon as Harding escorts the intruders back into

the hall, Mr. Levinson rushes to shut the door behind them—and locks the door. Then he turns his gaze to the back of the room. "Rae . . . ?"

Rae braces for some kind of lecture. But all her teacher says is: "Would you like to come to the board to help us work through the first problem?"

Rae sighs and heads for the board, thinking, *Maybe I should take another look at home schooling. . . .*

The whole day goes like that. At lunch Rae sits at her regular table with her friends and tries to ask Isobel about the math test.

But people keep interrupting. A lot of kids want to know when the contest is so they can go see Rae surf. Some of the guys stop to tease her, while a select few jocks from the football team unexpectedly cheer her on. But she's even more surprised when Andrea, the captain of the girls' varsity soccer team, stops by their table and holds out her yearbook. "Hey, Rae, how's it going? Can you sign my yearbook?"

Rae laughs, puzzled. "But, Andrea, that's last year's yearbook. The new ones aren't even out yet!"

"I know, I know. But man, you're my new hero. I know all the girls on the soccer team think it's really cool, what you're doing. You're a new pioneer for women in sports."

Rae is stunned. "Well, hey, all I did was accidentally get assigned to the wrong contest," she jokes.

"Yeah, none of this would have happened if her mom had named her Sue," Isobel jokes.

Andrea just shakes her head. "But you could have straightened all that out. You could have been a nice little girl and gone back to your side of the playground. But you didn't. It's like that woman golfer, Annika Sorenstam, who played in the PGA. A lot of people didn't want her there, didn't think it was right to let her play. But what she did was a huge step forward for all women athletes everywhere."

"Hey, Andrea, are you running for something, like student council?" Mick Davis, one of the football players, leans back in his chair from the next table.

"I think she should," Rae says. "You've got my vote, Andrea."

"She can be our first woman athlete president!" Isobel suggests.

Andrea laughs. "What can I say? This is all a big deal to me. Would you believe? My mom says when she was our age, her school didn't even have sports teams for girls. I mean, can you believe that? Nothing!"

"So now everything's fixed," Mick points out. "I mean, just about every girl I know is on some kind of team."

"Yeah, well, that didn't just happen," Andrea says. "Women of my mom's generation had to fight for it. And they're still *girls'* teams—they don't get the same money or the same publicity—"

"Or the same respect," Rae adds, getting fired up by Andrea's passion.

"Exactly."

"Hey, hey, I respect you all," Mick exclaims, holding up his hands. "'Cause I know Andrea here will beat me up if I don't!"

Andrea punches him in the arm. "Only on the field, man. Only on the field. I've gotta go get some lunch." She taps the yearbook on the table. "I'll pick up my autograph on the way out. But listen, good luck, Rae. A lot of your fans will be out there rooting for you."

"This is so cool, Rae," Cricket says. "Everybody in town is going to come see you surf."

"I guess. I just can't believe it," Rae replies. "All I wanted to do was surf. And maybe wipe that stupid grin off Chaz's face. I didn't realize I was going to be a cause."

That afternoon Rae has to help her mom with a trail ride. And for once she's glad not to be hitting the beach.

Rae doesn't mind horses, and she's a decent rider; she just doesn't get excited about them. Not like Sherri, who's like a Mini-Mom when it comes to horses. Rae will be glad when Mom can rely more on Sherri to help with the business and leave Rae to her waves.

That night at dinner Mom seems happier, maybe because Rae spent the afternoon on a horse without complaining. Dinner is almost like it used to be. Well, with one obvious exception. Dad.

But Mom seems in a good mood for a change, and Rae almost starts to tell her about all the things that happened at school. But something makes her hold back. Mom would like nothing better than to talk her into trading in her surfboard and flip-flops for a Western saddle and some riding boots.

After supper she goes online and finds an e-mail from her dad.

Hey, Rae of Sunshine—
Sorry I had to miss our IM date. I had a business dinner to attend and didn't get back in till late. Want to try again for 10 o'clock your time tonight? I miss you girls. Give Sherri a big hug for me.
Love, Dad

Rae can hardly wait! She drags out her books to study, but she keeps getting up to check the time. Her mom stops by her room and seems pleased to see her with her math book open.

At last it's almost time to go meet her dad online. But just as she signs on, her mom comes to the door. "Hey, don't you think it's about time for lights out?"

"But Mom," Rae says. "I got an e-mail from Dad today. He said he's going to IM me at ten!"

"Ten!" her mom exclaims. "On a school night? Absolutely not. What was he thinking?"

"But Mom," Rae protests. "I've been trying to meet up with him all week, and we just keep missing each other. And besides, all my friends stay up past—"

Rae freezes at her mom's look. The "all my friends" argument never works with her. So she simply says, "Just this once? I won't talk long, I promise. And I'll tell him that from now on I can't do it this late on a school night."

"Okay," her mom says reluctantly. "But keep it short."

Rae closes her door and checks her buddy list. Not there—wait! A bell chimes and her dad's screen name appears on her list.

Quickly she types an IM:

RAE: Dad! Hey! How R U?

DAD: Hey, Rae of Sunshine!

RAE: I was so glad to get your e-mail. Everything OK?

DAD: Yeah. Just a whole lot of work, that's all. And

RAE: R U still there?

DAD: Yeah. Sorry, that was just my cell phone. But I turned it off.

RAE: How R U? I miss U! So does Sherri.

DAD: I know. I miss you girls, too. How did you like the presents I sent?

RAE: Great!

DAD: And Sherri?

RAE: Sure. We miss you.

DAD: I miss you, too, sweetheart. I can't tell you how much. So what's going on?

Suddenly Rae blurts out everything—the contest, the mix-up, Chaz and his buddies. And how hard it is to have everybody staring at you and having an opinion about what you do. She wonders what he'll say. After all, he is a male. Will he think she's trying to mess things up?

But when she reads his reply, she breaks into a smile.

DAD: That's very cool, Rae!

RAE: Do you think I should do it? Do you think it's weird?

DAD: No! Go for it! You can do anything you want to, if you just put your mind to it. Go ahead. I'm proud of you!

The next day at school Rae keeps reminding herself about that IM session and what her dad said. It's the only way she can hold on through all the hype that's building up around her. People won't leave her alone. They either think she's great or they think she stinks. Either way they all have something to say.

Finally it's Rae's last period, a free period, which she usually spends in the library. This time she goes to the school nurse's office. Not because she's sick. Because she wants to get away, and the nurse, Mrs. Young, is a friend. She has a TV in the sickroom that plays softly all day. Rae thinks she'll go in there and catch a soap, forget her own problems for a while.

Instead the local news is on, and they're running her picture on the screen behind the anchor-person. There's a little news brief about her and then an interview—with none other than Chaz.

"It shouldn't be that big a deal," Rae is surprised to hear him say, until he adds, "Because she's going to get bombed on Day One. It's gotta happen. It's her first time competing at this level. It would be tough even if she was a guy".

"Interesting," the reporter says.

Rae makes a face at the TV. Did he actually say "even if she was a guy"? That's not interesting. It's stupid!

"Don't get me wrong," Chaz continues. "I'm not saying that surfers in the men's division are twice as good as surfers in the women's." Then he flashes a smile that half suggests he's teasing and doesn't really believe what he's saying, but Rae knows better. "I'm saying they're ten times better. Okay?"

"Not okay," Rae says to the TV. Mrs. Young comes in to watch, too.

"Strong stuff," the reporter says. "So how do you feel about your own chances?"

"I feel pretty good," Chaz says. "Remember, I grew up here. I've been surfing this place since the time I started walking. It's my beach."

"It's everybody's beach," Rae says.

"You tell him, Rae," Mrs. Young says.

Rae gives her a smile and gets up to leave. "I'll tell him," she says. "And show him. I'll show everybody."

When Rae leaves the school parking lot in her car she's followed by a van with TV-station call letters painted on its sides. She parks on the street because the beach access lot is full. Quickly she grabs a towel and her board off the roof rack and dodges the van while the driver looks for a parking place.

As soon as she sets foot on the beach she's aware of someone taping her. The van has let one of the crew loose with a Steadicam. Several other people with cameras who don't look like surfers spot the activity and start moving her way, too.

Then Drew appears.

"Hi, I've been waiting for you," he says. "Along with all these other people." He recognizes the look in her eyes. "Feel like getting out of here?"

"Is there a way?" Rae says.

"My car," he says. "I'm in a good getaway spot at the end of the access." Rae turns around and they stride off the beach together. The car is waiting. She straps her board on the roof rack and they take off.

"Where to?" he says when they're out of there.

"I was planning on doing some surfing," she says. "I'd still like to do that. Just not back there."

"What you need is a secret spot," he says. "And I know just the place." He turns the car off the beach road and takes a shortcut through a neighborhood of old vacation cottages that have yards now, with flowers and swing sets and dogs. They've become regular houses. The street comes to a bridge where the houses stop. On the other side there's a boatyard and then an empty lot where Rae can tell a gas station used to be. She doesn't know this part of town. It feels deserted.

Drew turns again and pulls into a parking lot beside a seafood restaurant with a big blue King Neptune out in front. It looks closed.

"Here?" Rae says.

"Secret spot," Drew says.

"I don't believe there's any surf here," Rae says.

"No one does. That's why it's a secret spot," Drew explains.

They take their boards off the roof of the car and Rae follows Drew around the side of the restaurant, past a Dumpster, to a high, solid wooden fence. He pushes open the gate and she follows him through it to an amazing, empty beach with beautifully shaped waves.

Neither one of them says a word, they just go out and surf.

After a while Drew goes in and sits on the beach. Then Rae catches a ride in, too, and they talk.

"I wonder if I'm doing the right thing," she says.

Drew shrugs. "You entered a surfing contest. What could be wrong with that?"

"You mean it started out that way."

"Yeah . . ."

"Now it's turned into something . . . huge."

"Not your fault."

"Maybe. Yesterday I saw a girl wearing a T-shirt that had my picture on it. It said 'RAE RULES.' Can you believe that? Wearing a T-shirt with my face on it!"

"Well, that's a compliment."

"I guess the problem I'm having is that none of this is about my surfing ability. It's all about the rule book. Which rules are right. Which rules are wrong. Your rules against my rules. Guy rules against Rae rules. Get it? Rae rules?"

"I think it's very cool what you're doing," Drew says.

Rae blushes. That's what her dad said, too.

What's my mom thinking? she wonders.

8

*T*he next morning Rae heads out at the crack of dawn looking for some audience-free board time. And to think about everything.

But even this early there's already a lone female surfer out there ahead of her.

Rae watches her—she's terrific technically, but also elegant, with a style all her own.

Rae heads out and finds her own place.

They take turns with the waves, the whole mood a world apart from the experience she had the day she shared—or rather, tried to share—the waves with Chaz and his buddies.

As the sun climbs higher in the sky, Rae paddles back in from a wave to find the woman sitting on her board in the trough, almost as if she's waiting for Rae. She's tall, lean like a ballerina, but strong-looking like a gymnast. Her long blond hair is pulled back into a braid. She looks like she's in her twenties.

"Hi," she says. "I'm Grace."

"I'm Rae."

Grace nods, smiling. "I've heard about you."

"You have?"

"Mm-hmm. You're causing quite a stir in the surfing world."

"I guess." Rae drags her hands through the water. "So what do you think about it all?"

"Hey, a little controversy's good for the sport. It wakes everybody up, you know?"

Rae laughs. "I guess!"

Grace stares off into the distance then. Rae can't tell if she's staring at the waves, or the beach, or something beyond, something else that's not even there. "Competition is a weird thing, you know? It can be a good thing . . . or a bad thing. Sometimes it can make us work harder, make us better . . . but sometimes . . ."

"Sometimes what?" Rae asks.

Grace grins like the Mona Lisa. "Sometimes it can become bigger than you, bigger than the entire ocean. Sometimes you can drown in it. And then you lose everything."

Rae is confused. She's not sure if Grace is telling her to compete against the guys or not. "So . . . what do you think I should do?"

Grace's clear blue eyes catch sight of the wave she wants, and she slips almost silently into the cool morning water. "What do I think?" She grins. "I think you should think what you want to think and not let all the attention mess with your head."

Rae sighs. "That sounds like a very long bumper sticker."

Grace laughs out loud. Then she asks, "Do you love to surf?"

"More than anything," Rae says.

"So surf. Surf alone or go play with the boys. But whatever you do, do it for yourself."

Grace is suddenly moving, paddling hard toward the challenge the next wave is offering her, and then she's up and flying.

It's one of the most beautiful things Rae has ever seen.

The next wave will be hers.

Rae decides to go for it.

That afternoon the tournament director holds a meeting of all the Division A surfers. It's unusual, but everyone's aware that the circumstances are not normal with Rae in the picture. The main speaker is the parks director and his message will be about behavior and the media. He wants to keep things under control.

When Rae shows up she spots Drew sitting near the front. He waves her over and she hurries to sit with him.

"Okay," the speaker begins, "I'm Doug Blande and I'm your parks director. I'd just like to say that we're very proud of you guys—uh, and lady—and we want you to have a lot of fun surfing out there with one another. That's what your parks department is here for. Fun. Okay? Now. We know there's a lot of publicity going on about this contest, and that's good, too. But we'd just like to ask everybody to kind of chill with the media on this. We don't want to cast a negative light on the wonderful sport of surfing and your parks department. Thank you."

And there's a round of halfhearted applause.

The tournament director gets up next. "I'd like to add that some of our sponsors are worried about the wrong message getting out and hurting the event. Maybe even the whole sport."

"They oughta be!" Rae hears someone call out near the front.

"Is that Chaz?" she whispers.

"Yeah." Drew shakes his head. "What's that guy's problem anyway?"

"I don't know, I can't figure him out," Rae says. "It's like it goes beyond the girl-guy thing."

A lot of people in the crowd have comments or questions. But then Chaz speaks up again. "So when are you going to give the guys back their contest?"

"Somebody needs to put a muzzle on that guy," Drew says in disgust. Then he gives Rae a long indecipherable look and says, "Maybe it should be me."

Rae grabs his arm. "Drew!" she whispers. "What are you doing?"

Drew smiles at her reassuringly, then turns toward the crowd. "I just want to say that I think most of these comments are ridiculous. First of all, this controversy is hardly hurting the sport. If anything, it's attracting a lot of media attention—and attracting people who don't usually watch the sport. That's good for all of us. And I, for one, think we're focusing too much energy on the wrong things. I mean, come on. Are we guy surfers? Or girl surfers? Or just surfers?"

"Well, if you don't know, I'm not going to help you find out!" Chaz wisecracks. But he doesn't get many laughs.

Rae smiles as she realizes people are really listening to Drew.

"I don't need any help figuring it out," Drew goes on. "I know what's important here. And that's the feeling I share with anybody who understands this strange passion we have for a surfboard. Anybody who wakes up in the morning with one thought: How are the waves today? All of us who think like that—male or female—should just focus on our love of the sport and the bonds that make us a community. I think we should let Rae—or anybody else who qualifies—surf in this or any other contest."

"Well, sure," Chaz snaps. "The only reason that you care is that she's your *girlfriend*."

Rae winces. How embarrassing. She glances up at Drew. She hopes this doesn't make him hate her forever.

"Well, not exactly," he says, "we're just getting to know each other, really. But I'd consider myself pretty lucky if she was my girlfriend. Because she's a great surfer, and a tough competitor. And I think it will be great to surf in competition against her."

Okay. Rae is mush. Drew is unbelievable. She liked this guy a whole lot already; now she's totally nuts about him.

When he sits down, he smiles and gives her hand a little squeeze.

"Thanks," she says softly.

"Hey, thank you," he says with a grin.

"What did I do?"

"I've been surfing for a long time," he says. "But what you've done has really made me think about everything and figure out how I feel about surfing." He winks. "And a few other things."

Rae is staring into Drew's gorgeous eyes, wondering if she can stop herself from giving this guy a huge kiss right in front of everybody, when Doug steps up to the mike. "The sponsors have made their decision," he announces.

Rae holds her breath.

"Rae Perrault can surf in any division she wants."

The crowd erupts in cheers and arguments.

With a shout, Drew scoops Rae up into his arms and swings her around in a circle the way her dad used to do when she was little. Sort of.

So, Rae decides as she slips her arms around Drew's neck, *who's gonna notice one little kiss in all this commotion?*

9

*T*hen everything goes wrong. Suddenly.

It starts with some graffiti on Rae's surfboard. She cleans it off. It happens again. Her friends help her this time.

"It's just some kids," Kanani says.

"I'd like to catch 'em," Luna says.

"In the act," Isobel adds.

"I'd like to paint them up and see how they like scrubbing this off," Cricket says.

So Rae has to watch her board more closely. She locks it up inside the car instead of leaving it up on the cartop rack. She feels like she needs to have it with her more.

Then she gets the letter. It comes in a plain white envelope, neatly typed on a computer, obviously, and printed out. No handwriting to trace. All it says is:

DROP OUT OF THE COMPETITION. NOW. OR ELSE. FROM, A CONCERNED SURFER

The letter comes to the house, where Rae's mom sees it, and freaks out.

"A threatening note! We have your father to thank for this!" she shouts.

Sherri is shocked. "Dad? What does he have to do with this?"

"Rae, I've always had this fear of you getting caught up in those waves," Mom says. "The ocean is deceptive, it's a force more powerful than we are. You could drown, for God's sake! But he's always supported you in the hobby. Said it was 'cool.' Now look what's happening. You're being threatened! I don't want to see a grudge carried out against you in the water."

This last bit of reasoning escapes Rae. "You argued about surfing?"

"Sweetheart, your father and I argued about *everything*. Did we argue about surfing? Yes. Of course! Why not!"

The phone rings, and Sherri rushes to pick it up. When the phone's off the hook, she knows, Mom won't yell. It's for her anyway.

"It's the high school," Sherri says.

Now what? Rae thinks.

The call is on their cordless phone, so Mom can walk out of the room where they can't hear. In a few minutes she's back with bad news.

"That was your math teacher, Rae. Midterm progress reports are coming out, and your grade has dropped a whole point. I set up a conference for the three of us. On Saturday."

"Saturday?" Rae gasps, incredulous.

"This Saturday," Mom says firmly.

"But Saturday's the competition. I can't do it!"

"Get your priorities straight, young lady," Mom snaps back. "Your grades are more important than a competition that's gotten out of control. Consider your surfing days over."

10

"*T*hat's not fair!" Rae says. "After all I've gone through and all the attention I've had to deal with. . . . Now I can't even be in the event at all?"

"It's just a surfing contest," her mom says. "God knows, there'll be plenty of others—"

"Not like this one!" Rae is so upset she's shaking. "Mom—girl surfers everywhere are counting on me!"

"Well, I'm counting on you to go to your room and open that math book!" her mom replies angrily. "Subject closed." Her mother heads out the back door. Rae knows her horses will be getting a vigorous grooming tonight.

Furious, Rae heads to her room and locks her door. She opens her math book—just like her mom said. But she doesn't look at it. Instead she signs on to her computer to see if any of her friends are online. She's got to talk to someone!

But none of them are on. She sends a brief e-mail telling them what's happened. Then her dad shows up on her buddy list! Rae immediately sends him a "need to talk" IM.

DAD: What's wrong, Rae of Sunshine?

And then everything comes pouring out. All about the surfing contest, everything she's been going through. Dad does a lot of listening, but instead of coming down on her, like Mom, he tells her to hang on to her dream.

RAE: How can I? Mom says I have to quit.
DAD: Quit surfing?
RAE: Immediately.
DAD: What about the competition?
RAE: I'll be going to a teacher conference that day.
DAD: I'll see what I can do.
RAE: No, Dad.

But he's offline.

Later that night the phone rings and Rae knows it's him. Mom answers, then doesn't say anything for what seems like a long time. She walks over to Rae's door and shuts it. Then she hears Sherri's door close. Then Mom's voice fades away as she walks into her own bedroom with the phone and shuts that door.

There's only one thing worse than having your parents separate, Rae thinks.

Having them fight over you.

The next morning Rae wakes up hoping her mom's anger has blown over and she'll get to compete. She opens her door to the smell of pancakes on the stove.

That's a good sign, she thinks.

Sherri comes out of the bathroom, brushing her teeth. She waggles her hand "hi."

Okay . . . Rae thinks.

She sits down at the kitchen counter. "Good morning, Mom."

"Good morning," Mom says. "Finish your math homework?"

"Yes," Rae says.

"Good." She flips a pancake over. The suspense is killing Rae. Finally Mom delivers the final, crushing blow. "Come straight home after school, will you? I want to go over it with you."

Instead of going surfing, Rae thinks.

Rae eats and gets ready for school. On her way out, her mom reminds her about the teacher conference.

"I won't forget," Rae says.

At school, everyone's talking about the competition. Some of the boys tell Rae "You're gonna get wiped!" Girls are saying it's the boys who are in for a thrashing. Rae doesn't have the heart to tell them that her mom has scrubbed her from the competition. She just keeps hoping that something good will happen. She keeps hanging on to her dream.

In math class, there's a glimmer of hope. Her math teacher, Mr. Levinson, apologizes. "I completely forgot about the competition when I spoke to your mom, Rae," he says. "I left a message on your answering machine asking if we could change it to this afternoon instead. I hope she gets it."

"Me, too," Rae says. At lunch there's a message at the office for Rae, from her mom. She got Mr. Levinson's message and she'll meet Rae there right after school.

"You must be very proud of Rae," Mr. Levinson says to Rae's mom when he meets her.

"Yes, I am," her mom replies.

"The reason I called you both in is only for precautionary reasons. Rae is a good student. But math is something we have to"—and here he raises two fingers of each hand, and bounces them, making quotation marks—"keep up with."

Rae's mom nods.

"There is a popular myth about girls when it comes to math," he continues. "People sometimes say girls aren't good at math. That's simply not true. We don't want Rae to buy into that and stop trying."

"I have to admit math wasn't my best subject," Rae's mom says.

"Would you believe I was the same way in my early

years in school?" Mr. Levinson says. "Yet look at me now. I teach math!"

"But you're a guy," Rae says.

"Good point," Mr. Levinson says. "Does it disprove my theory? Not if you consider who tutored me in the subject. It was my mother. She was a math teacher, too."

"That's pretty cool," Rae says.

"I feel a lot better about this," her mom tells Mr. Levinson.

"I'm sure everything will be on track by the end of the semester. Just keep up with the exercises." Then Mr. Levinson smiles. "Between sets, that is."

"What?" For a moment Rae thinks he was talking about number sets. Then she realizes he meant surfing.

"Do you surf as well, Mrs. Perrault?" Mr. Carter asks Rae's mom.

"I . . . no," she stammers. "That is, Rae's the surfer in the family. She's fearless in the water."

"She's made quite a reputation for herself," he says. "Again, you must be very proud. And I apologize for almost forgetting Saturday's competition." Mr. Levinson stands up and extends his hand to Rae's mom. "I hope I'll see you there!"

Rae's mom reaches out and shakes his hand. "Yes. I hope so, too!" She glances at Rae, then looks back at the math teacher. "Thank you for everything."

Rae grabs Mr. Levinson's hand and shakes it vigorously. "Yes, thank you so much!" she said.

* * *

"Mom? Did I hear right?"

"What?" They are walking to the parking lot together.

"Did you tell Mr. Levinson you'd see him at the beach tomorrow? Are you going to the competition? Am I?"

"Well . . ." Rae's mom says.

"Oh, come on, Mom. Please. I got a great idea while we were in there. I know a girl who's in college. She's a total brain. And she's a surfer, too, Mom. You can be both, you know."

"You think?"

"Mom," Rae pleaded. "Listen to me. Her name is Grace. I met her while I was surfing the other day. She goes to college back East but she's here now and she knows algebra the way you know horses. I know she'll tutor me. I'll catch up, Mom. I promise."

Rae's mom sighs and scans the parking lot. "Now where did I park?"

"Mom, you're not listening."

"Yes I am."

"Mom."

"Oh, there it is. The car's over there." She points. Rae looks and sees her mom's car. There's a surfboard on top.

Rae's surfboard.

"I thought when our appointment got changed you might need it," her mom says.

Rae gives her a big hug.

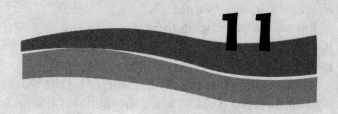

11

*R*ae carries her board in its nylon cover down to the beach. It's early but the tournament officials are already set up. There's a scoring table and down the beach three folding chairs for the judges spaced far enough apart so they won't talk or influence each other. A guy in a bright orange windbreaker with the letters *BC* on the back—for *beach coordinator*—is pointing at the water as he talks with an older man whom Rae recognizes as the tournament director.

Conditions are good: five-foot waves under a starry sky that's fading to blue as the sun rises.

Rae puts her board down and heads for the water. She wades in up to her knees. It feels cool and inviting.

"Hey, it's another perfect day," someone says. "How typical." It's Drew. He never gets tired of complimenting the weather in California.

"The water isn't bad, either," Rae says. "We should see some good scores today."

Drew nods. As a competitive surfer, he's well aware that when conditions are poor, judges become subjective. Less fair, some would say.

Rae wants the scoring to be as fair as possible. She hopes the fact that she's "breaking in" to the men's competition doesn't turn any of the judges off.

A whistle blows. A crowd has gathered on the beach. It's almost seven o'clock, when the first heat is scheduled to begin.

The BC motions for all the surfers to meet at the scoring table. Rae and Drew join the crowd that's gathered there. Rae sees a lot of surfers she doesn't know. Plus Chaz and his buddies.

"Okay," the BC says. "The judges will be using a twenty-point system, so there's lots of room for accuracy and scoring on everything you put into your ride: choice of wave, tricks, style. Over two hundred surfers applied for this little competition, and only twelve guys were accepted. You're a small group of highly skilled athletes. All of you have a lot to be proud of just by making the cut. All twelve of you will get to show your stuff twice today—once in the morning and once in the afternoon. The top nine will compete again in four heats tomorrow and then it's down to three guys grabbing for the glory." Suddenly he seems to notice Rae for the first time. "Excuse me. Three persons grabbing for the glory."

For just a second everyone looks over at Rae. Most of the expressions are polite, or at least noncommittal.

Except Chaz. He glares at her, openly. Rae concentrates on the BC, ignoring him.

"We'll have four heats today, made up of three surfers each, giving you plenty of room and no need for interference calls, okay?" Like Rae, the BC is looking for a clean contest, without a lot of arguments over the rules. He consults his clipboard and reads the names for the first heat—Drew and two other surfers Rae doesn't know. They walk to the water with their boards and paddle out. When they're seated on the swell, the scorekeeper winds a kitchen timer to twenty minutes and puts up a green flag.

It's on.

The first wave rolls through without a rider. The second one, which to Rae looks identical, gets a taker. It's one of the surfers she doesn't know. He's good. He chases the peak and drops onto the wave and goes almost straight down, for maximum speed. He pulls out at the last minute and carves a zigzag across the face of it. There's a lot of cheering from the beach. The contest is off to a good start.

A second rider goes in on the next wave and stays on it all the way to the shore break, a great long ride. There's more applause from the beach. Then it's Drew's turn. He lets a wave go by and then catches a big barrel-shaped roller.

Wisely, instead of speeding out of the trough like the surfers before him, he makes a slower, smooth turn out of the trough, letting the tube catch up and cover him. From the beach, the waterfall makes him look like a shadow in the wave. When the barrel squeezes down, he emerges and makes an effortless-looking exit over the top of the crest.

"Awesome! Go, Drew!" Rae yells. For getting covered up, and with points for style, she thinks he's probably scored the best in the first heat. The timer on the scoring table rings and the BC blows his whistle for the next gang of three to assemble for heat number two. Chaz is in this one, too, along with someone named Sean. And Rae.

The BC checks their names off and reminds them to look for the green flag before they go.

Heading for the water, Rae finds out she's got a fan club of local girls who've showed up to support her. They do the name cheer—"R-A-E: What's that spell?"—and the crowd perks up and answers, "Rae!" Then the cheerleaders roar, "Yay!" and Rae can see that really burns Chaz. He glares over his shoulder, then duck-dives through a wave on his way out to sea.

As she sits on the swell, the water feels cushiony, like a gentle pony ride. Rae feels like she's going into a trance. The beach is moving up and down, up and down. It's a state she goes into before every competitive ride. Total relaxation.

"Ladies first," Chaz says, razzing her.

Rae guesses Sean, the other surfer out there, thinks Chaz is being polite, but she knows what he's being is fake. "Get over it, Chaz," she complains, then thinks, *Calm down. Don't let him get to you.*

Chaz's remark doesn't mean Rae's going to let him go first. In fact, the first wave in the set is the one she wants. She starts to take off when suddenly Chaz practically runs her over. It startles her and she gets out of the way. He takes the wave.

Rae can't tell from where she sits what kind of ride Chaz has, but the reaction from the crowds looks good. Not spectacular, but good. She knows he didn't wipe out. Then Rae glances behind her at the next wave, and it looks like another good one. She gives Sean a look that says this one is hers and digs in after the peak, then comes out on the wave feeling like she's riding the top of a freight train. She drops down the face of the wave steeply and carves out just as it starts to break behind her. The roaring sound catches up to her and the water changes color from blue to deep green as the wave covers her up.

Bam! It feels like the fin struck something in the water and she crashes into the wall. The circular motion of the water drags her around the tube and the only thing she remembers later about what happened after that is how she kept looking for the board, trying to stay out of its way.

She knows it's over when she feels the bottom and can stop herself and stand up. She ends up facing the beach and her board, which is waiting for her like a dog for its master. She waves at the anxious crowd on the beach. "I'm okay!" she yells, and they give her a round of applause. She smiles, but that's only on the outside. Inside she's thinking, *That wipeout is going to kill my score.*

To stay in the contest, she'll have to be brilliant this afternoon.

12

"**Y**ou looked like you were trying to kill that wave, Rae," Jeremy, one of the other guys in the competition, tells her. Jeremy, Rae, and Drew are having a light lunch under an umbrella table outside the 7th Street Pavilion, a restaurant overlooking the beach.

"Thank you for being honest," she replies.

"Everybody feels the pressure at these things," he goes on. "You're carrying an extra load breaking in as a girl surfer. It might be too much. For anyone, not just you, Rae."

"Come on, we've all had our wipeouts," Drew reminded him.

"Of course we have," Jeremy says. "What I meant was . . . in Rae's case . . ." But he's not sure how to finish.

"What he meant was, in Rae's case, it's time to shut it down." It's Chaz. He puts his plate down and takes a seat at their table.

Rae looks at him askance. "Well, why don't you join us," she says.

"Don't mind if I do," Chaz replies. He shrugs his head at the tables behind them. "All the other seats are taken, okay? You're almost finished anyway."

"You know everything, don't you, Chaz," Rae says.

"No, not everything," he mumbles, his mouth full of food. "But yes, some things. Some things very well. Like for example, the fact that you're not welcome here. I know that. You don't seem to get it, though. So I'll explain it for you. It's nothing personal. This is just not a women's event. You're showing disrespect for the division."

"I'm showing my interest in competing at a higher level," Rae shoots back. "That's not disrespect." Rae feels like she's the one who's being dissed. Not the other way around.

"I'm talking about what it looks like to everyone else," Chaz says. "Okay, maybe you're thinking 'Rae's doing the right thing. Rae's being the best surfer she can be.' Problem is, everybody else is saying 'Rae wants the spotlight. She doesn't care if she turns Division A into a circus.' You're quite famous now. More famous than you'd ever be on the basis of your surfing."

Rae feels like slapping him, and almost does. The only thing that stops her is someone else's hand on her shoulder. Looking up, she sees a man wearing a navy blue golf shirt, a Yankees baseball cap, and a warm smile. She can't believe it.

"Dad!"

"Live and in person," he says.

Rae stands up and gives him a hug. "What are you doing here?" she says.

Jake Perrault chuckles. "Let me look at you," he says, holding her at arms' length.

"Your shirt," Rae says. There's sand on it, from hugging her. She brushes it off.

"I had some vacation time saved up," he tells her. "Couldn't think of a better way to spend it than watching you compete."

"Did you see me wipe out?" Rae says, wincing.

"I did. But I understand you have another chance this afternoon."

Rae shakes her head and smiles. "You should have told me you were here," she says.

"My plane was a little late," he tells her. "And I didn't want to make waves, so to speak. But I'm letting you know now. You have one more fan cheering you on."

Rae and her dad walk down the beach together, where he's set himself up with a rented cabana chair.

"Nice digs, Dad," Rae comments.

"It's comfy," he says. "And it's got great views." The competition area is right in front of him. The water sparkles in the sun, contrasting with the dark rollers crashing against the beach.

Drew's words come back to her. It really is a perfect day.

She feels like making the most of it.

Rae's second ride is scheduled for the third afternoon heat. Chaz is in with her, again. The BC calls them together—Rae, Chaz, and another young surfer who goes by the name Mojo—for the preheat instructions.

The BC's speech is just like the morning one, with a caution thrown in for Rae's benefit, no doubt.

"Don't want to see anybody gettin' hurt out there," he says.

"Of course not!" Chaz says, grinning at Rae.

Rae doesn't let it bother her. She's feeling good as they paddle out. The water feels even better now that the sun has warmed things up. The presence of her dad on the beach makes her feel less like a stranger here.

What hasn't changed is Chaz. Out of the water, Rae thinks of him as a minor irritation. He's a joke, really. But in the water he can be dangerous. Rae knows she doesn't want to be on the same wave with Chaz the way she was that first morning they met.

This time when the first wave comes, Rae moves quickly, blocking Chaz.

"Hey!" he yells.

She doesn't appear to hear him. Rae paddles hard and catches the wave just behind the peak, a good scoring move that will increase her speed on the wave, as well. She makes a smooth entry, an almost vertical drop into the trough, pulls out, and cuts a pattern up and down across the wave. She feels light and totally in control as she rides the lip over and back inside again.

She stays on the wave until it exhausts itself, then gracefully hops off and stops the board in the water.

She turns her head just in time to see Chaz wipe out.

There's one more wipeout that day, but it doesn't happen anywhere near the beach. Rae's dad comes to the house for dinner. Things start out okay. Then the competition begins.

"So how are you girls enjoying the new laptop computer?" Dad says. Rae and Sherri trade a look. They're afraid to answer. Afraid of Mom. No problem, though. She answers for them.

"Oh, they're enjoying it very much. Of course, it'll be out of date by the time either of them is in college. I wonder if you thought about putting that money in a college fund?"

"It wasn't that expensive," he says.

"Not to you. You're a single person."

It goes on like that for a few minutes and then gets very quiet. The only sound is the noise of forks touching the plates.

Then Sherri says, "How come Rae got a computer and all I got was a digital camera?"

And it is all over.

"Good night, Jake," Mom says. "Girls, go to your rooms."

"I'm supposed to meet Drew," Rae whispers.

Mom glares at her. "Fine! Go!"

13

*R*ae's board is still on the car rack when she pulls into the parking lot in front of the coffee shop. Drew's there waiting for her.

"Couldn't miss you," he says about the board on the car.

"Oh, I know," she says. "I left the house kind of fast."

"There is surf at night," Drew adds. "At least that's what I've heard. How about a decaf?"

"Sounds good," Rae says, and they go inside.

A few minutes later they're coming back for an outside table and Drew spots someone standing beside Rae's car.

"Who is that?" he says. Then shouts, "Hey!"

The guy by the car is Chaz. Rae and Drew walk out to meet him.

"What are you doing, man?" Drew asks.

"Nothing," Chaz says.

Obviously lying, Rae thinks.

"Messing with Rae's board? Scribbling on it, maybe?"

Chaz looks over at the board. "What are you talking about? This is Rae's board?"

"You know it is," Drew says.

"I had no idea," Chaz says. "I was just looking at it."

"Okay, look," Drew says. "This has gone far enough. Let's talk this out. Chaz? Come on. I'll buy you a cup."

Chaz frowns. "I can buy my own," he says.

"Okay, that's cool," Drew says. "Let's go, man."

A few minutes later the three of them are at a table in front of the coffee shop.

"What's the deal, Chaz?" Drew says. "Does it really bother you that much that Rae's in the showdown? Do you really think she actually represents any competition whatsoever to someone with your ability?"

Rae gives Drew an offended look.

"Hang with me here, Rae," he says.

Chaz frowns. "I think I've made my opinion pretty clear."

"No doubt," Drew says. "But I'm looking for what's behind that opinion."

Rae sees where this is going. "If you're right about me, that I'm so not up to your level, why do you care? It doesn't make sense, Chaz."

"Doesn't make sense. You sound like my sister," Chaz snaps.

"Your sister?"

"She's an amazing surfer. She could have gone pro, easy," Chaz tells them. "But she's smart, too, so she chose to go to an Ivy League college instead."

"And you didn't," Rae surmises.

"Right," Chaz confirms. "I didn't have anywhere near the grades she had. And that's something I'll never forget, because my parents won't ever let me. I don't have my sister's smarts, even though I'm good out there"—he jabs his thumb at what all three surfers know instinctively is the direction of the sea— "I'll never be as good as her at anything in their eyes. I don't want to compete with her anymore."

"That's okay with me," Rae says. "I'm not your sister."

Chaz looks down at the pavement. For a minute they're all quiet. "I know."

Then he says something amazing. "I'm sorry, Rae."

An hour later, when they're ready to leave, Drew offers Chaz a ride home, and Rae goes along for the ride. When they get to Chaz's place, Grace is there, on the porch.

"Speak of the devil," Chaz jokes.

"Grace?" Rae says.

"You've already met?" Chaz asks.

"Well, yeah," Rae says. "We just talked on the phone today."

"I'm her math tutor," Grace says. "How do you two know each other?"

"It's a long story," Drew says. He looks at Rae. "Why don't we leave? Tomorrow's a big day. Gotta get some shut-eye."

Rae nods. She knows Chaz and Grace have some catching up to do. "Okay, just give me a lift back to my car," she says.

"I'll do better than that," Drew promises. "Your place is on the way to mine. I'll follow you. We're not going to let anything happen to you the day before the tournament."

"That's an offer I can't refuse," Rae says.

It's a good thing she doesn't. At Rae's house, all the lights are on, inside and out. And there are flashlights in the woods.

Rae jumps out of her car. "Mom! What is it? What's up?" she yells.

Rae's mom runs to her with a worried look on her face.

"It's Sherri! She's disappeared!"

14

"We're going across the road," a man says. Rae recognizes the voice as her dad's.

"We've been looking almost since you left," Rae's mom tells her. "The neighbors are out, too."

"What happened?" Drew asks.

"I don't know, exactly," her mom says. Rae can see she feels guilty. "Your father and I were talking about something. I don't remember what it was about. Arguing, probably.

"Anyway, I called Sherri to help clear the table, and she wasn't in her room. We've been looking ever since. I'm going across the road with your father. Check around here, maybe we missed something." Then she leaves.

Rae turns to Drew. "It's my fault. Our mom and dad were quarreling at dinner. I bagged it. Left to meet you. I didn't even think about Sherri being stuck here."

"We'll find her," Drew says. "I used to run away all the time when I was a kid. Eventually, my mom and dad stopped looking for me. Kind of took the fun out of it, so I gave it up."

Rae laughs. "You may be right. She's probably right under our noses."

"Does your house have a basement?"

"No," Rae says. "There's this crawl space underneath, but I don't think Sherri would go there. She doesn't like bugs."

"Hmm. What about a storage shed?"

"There's a lawnmower shed, but it smells like gasoline. She wouldn't go there."

"Do you have a doghouse?"

"No, Drew. Plus she wouldn't hide in a doghouse. Fleas. Remember?"

"Right. Bugs. What about the attic?"

"Hmmm . . . too much dust. Besides, Mom would have checked there, I think."

"Inside, maybe, but what about outside?" Rae follows as Drew circles the house and looks up to see a small opening with mini French doors spread wide. "Do you always keep that window open?"

Rae follows his hand as he gestures toward the rooftop where two tiny legs capped with long-laced sneakers jut out from behind the fiberglass-hooded roof fan. She smiles. "Never. Except maybe sometimes."

"Ah-hah," he says, his voice growing louder. "And do you suppose the dust bunnies up there in the attic get restless and decide to go outside for some fresh air once in a while?"

Rae laughs. "Could be," she shouts back as they move closer to the side of the house where they can see Sherri's face in the moonlight.

"Why, look, I think I see a little dust bunny now!" he says, pointing to Sherri in mock surprise.

"How did you know I was up here?" Sherri finally says, calling down to them.

"One of my favorite hiding places," Drew says. "No one ever thinks of it. They look down, around, and even below, but they often forget to look up."

"Sherri, I'm so glad you're okay," Rae says. "We have to tell Mom and Dad. And the entire neighborhood."

Sherri looks worried. "Am I in trouble?"

"A little, maybe," Rae says. "But it'll be okay. I'll be your lawyer."

Soon Rae and Drew convince Sherri to join them on the ground. They stand by, ready to catch Sherri in case she falls, as she climbs down the rose trellis. Then Rae grabs hold of her and hugs her sister. "Why did you run off and hide from everybody like that?" she asks.

"Because," Sherri says. "Dad still thinks I'm a baby. He hasn't been gone long but I've grown up a lot lately, you know? And Mom only gets mad at you."

Rae looks puzzled. "You want Mom to get mad at you?"

"She gets mad because she's worried. I want her to worry about me, too."

Rae grabs her and holds her tight.

Two more people join them at the side of the house. It's Rae and Sherri's mom and dad.

"We *were* worried about you, Sherri," Mom says. Rae turns her sister over to Mom and Dad so they can hug her, too.

"Hey, sister," Rae says. "You want to have a sleepover in my room tonight?"

Sherri just grins.

15

On Sunday, the crowd on the beach has doubled from the day before, and a lot of the newcomers are females. The cheerleaders are back, and Rae's happy and a little bit stunned to see her mom and sister cheering along with them. Sherri's holding a poster she made that says RAE RULES, hoping to catch the eye of a surfing-magazine photographer. Rae sees a scene she wishes she had a picture of: Chaz's sister, Grace, is there, and she's obviously giving Chaz surfing advice. Rae catches her eye and Grace gives her a thumbs-up.

"How are you feeling?" Rae says when she spots Drew.

Drew's face brightens. "As just another plain old guy surfer, I'm feeling pretty ordinary. How are you feeling?"

"Overrated," Rae says, with a smile. "I mean, I made the finals. People are acting like I won."

"You did win," Drew says. "You got in the tournament on account of your ability as a surfer. You stayed in the game and beat surfers at a high level of competition. With no support from your fellow competitors."

"You've been very supportive, Drew."

"Right. I forgot about that. Except me."

"And my mom and dad are here. My sister."

"The cheerleaders."

"That's right! And all those other women who've showed up to support me! You guys should be thanking me."

"You've done a lot for the tournament just being here, Rae. But frankly, I'll be glad when the circus is over. And we can get back to surfing for surfing's sake."

"I hear you," Rae says. "But I have to tell you I am looking forward to the heats."

There's been a change in the schedule. The tournament director has moved Rae from one of the early heats to number four, the last one in the semifinals before the tournament top three compete. He's saving her for last.

In the first heat, Jeremy's in top form. He demolishes the competition with another stunning ride inside the curl. In the third heat, Chaz makes up for his wipeout the day before. Rae thinks he's probably going on to the finals. In the fourth heat, Rae catches a fast-moving wave and carves strong, graceful turns across the face. It's a good ride—not quite enough to put her in the finals—but that's okay. Her final scores put her ahead of four other semifinalists. It's a great showing for someone who entered in a higher level of competition for the first time—male or female.

In the finals, Jeremy takes the title again. Chaz is second, then the surfer from Rae's first round, Sean.

"Congratulations," Rae says to Chaz.

"Thanks." He grins. She's never seen him so genuine. "See you next time?"

Rae smiles. "Maybe."

That night Rae's family goes out to dinner to celebrate. It's been an amazing twenty-four hours. Rae made her way to the finals in a Division A tournament. Sherri got lost and found. And Rae and Sherri's mom and dad have actually started getting along for a change. At one point, Rae even sees them laugh. Together. It makes her feel just the slightest bit hopeful.

"Ladies," her dad says, when they're seated at a table. "I want to tell you I feel like the luckiest man alive to have two wonderful daughters like you. Thank you for being who you are. And I also want to thank your mother for making you both possible."

"Now it's my turn," Rae's mom says. "I want to say that your father and I have talked about this, and we both agree that we owe you two an apology . . . for the strain we've put you under. We've been thinking a great deal about ourselves, and our own struggle with our marriage, and not enough about how it must be affecting you.

"Neither one of us wants to lose your love. And so we get overly competitive with each other at times. But deep down, it's like that surfing contest today. We both want the same thing. Happy and safe lives; a good ride for both of you."

The waiter arrives and everybody orders.

"Are you coming to my tap recital?" Sherri asks her dad.

"It's in May, right?" he says. "Already got it on my calendar. You guys should come out and visit me sometime, too. If your mom can spare you for a week." He looks at Mom.

Rae looks at her, too.

"I think we can work something out," she says.

After dinner they stop at the 7th Street access for ice cream and a walk down the beach. The scoring table, the judges' chairs, the people—the tournament—it's all disappeared. The tide has even washed away the footprints. It's all brand-new.

Up ahead, Rae's mom and dad are walking together. Rae and Sherri stop to skip shells on the ocean.

It's hard for Rae not to think about what if—

What if they could all come back together as a family? It's something that may or may not happen. Time only knows.

For now, she remains hopeful, and glad just to be having a good time on the beach.